James and the Giant Peach

LEVEL 6

Re-told by: Jocelyn Potter
Series Editor: Melanie Williams

Pearson Education Limited
Edinburgh Gate, Harlow,
Essex CM20 2JE, England
and Associated Companies throughout the world.

ISBN: 978-1-4479-3137-9

This edition first published by Pearson Education Ltd 2014

3 5 7 9 10 8 6 4 2

Set in 15/19pt OT Fiendstar
Printed in China
SWTC/02

Published by Pearson Education Ltd

For a complete list of the titles available in the Pearson English Kids Readers series, please go to
www.pearsonenglishkidsreaders.com. Alternatively, write to your local Pearson Education office or to
Pearson English Readers Marketing Department, Pearson Education, Edinburgh Gate, Harlow, Essex CM20 2JE, England.

CHAPTER 1

When he was young, James Trotter had a very comfortable life with his parents in a beautiful house beside the sea. He had a lot of friends, and they played happily together on the beach.

Then, one day, James's mother and father went shopping in London and had a terrible accident. A large angry rhinoceros escaped from London Zoo and – on a busy street, in the middle of the day – it ate James's parents.

Their problems ended, of course, when they died. But James was alone now, so he had to live with two horrible aunts.

Aunt Sponge and Aunt Spiker were lazy, greedy and *very* unkind. From the first day, they shouted at James, and they hit him for almost no reason. They did not give him toys or picture books, and they never took him anywhere.

James's aunts lived on the top of a hill in the middle of nowhere, and there was nothing in their garden except one old peach tree. Poor James could not leave the garden, and he never saw other children. He became sadder and sadder, and more and more lonely.

CHAPTER 2

Three years later, something strange happened. James was cutting wood for the kitchen fire, and the work was making him hot, tired and unhappy. Suddenly, a strange old man stood in front of him. In his hand, the old man held a white bag.

'Look inside!' he told James.

James was very frightened, but he looked into the bag. Bright little green things that looked like stones moved around inside it!

'There's more magic in those little stones than in all the world,' the old man said. 'Take them! They're yours. They'll make you happy.'

Excited, James ran towards the house. But he ran too fast and he fell.

The bag burst open under the old peach tree and the little green things went everywhere. Then they disappeared into the ground.

'Where are they?' James thought. 'And what will happen to their magic?'

Then he heard Aunt Spiker's voice. 'Look, sister! It's a peach!'

'But that tree never has any peaches,' Aunt Sponge answered.

'It's got one now – and it's growing in front of my eyes!'

The peach grew bigger and bigger, and heavier and heavier.

'Will it ever stop growing?' Aunt Sponge shouted. 'This can't continue!'

But it did not stop.

When the bottom of the peach reached the ground, James's aunts walked around it.
It was lovely – yellow, pink and red.

'I've never seen a more beautiful thing,' James thought.

Aunt Sponge touched it carefully.

'It's perfect,' she said happily. 'Let's cut off a piece and eat it.'

'No,' Aunt Spiker said with a greedy smile. 'Not yet. We can make some money from this peach. I've got a plan!'

Soon everyone heard the news about the giant peach. The aunts locked James in his bedroom when crowds of visitors arrived.

'Pay before you look!' they shouted at the gate.

They took a lot of money.

At the end of the day, they opened James's door.

'Clean the garden!' they told him. 'Those people have dropped food and paper everywhere.'

James stood in the dark and looked at the giant peach, a ball of silver in the moonlight. He walked slowly towards it and touched it. It felt soft and warm.

Suddenly, he noticed a hole in the peach.

CHAPTER 3

James stepped into the hole. The floor was wet, and peach juice ran down from the ceiling into his mouth. It tasted delicious.

He came to a wall – the stone in the middle of the peach! He opened a small door and walked inside.

A voice said, 'Here he is!'

Another voice said, 'You're late!'

Very frightened, James looked at the speakers.

In front of him was a group of giant insects. Each insect was as big as James.

Miss Spider looked at James and said, 'I'm hungry!'

'I am too!' the Old-Green-Grasshopper said.

'And me!' the Ladybird cried.

'Aren't *you* hungry?'
Miss Spider asked James,
and he felt better.
They did not want
to eat *him*!

'Welcome, James!'
the Old-Green-
Grasshopper said.

'Can you help
me with
these boots?' the
Centipede asked.

'You're wearing
a *lot* of boots,'
James said.

'I've got a hundred legs!' the Centipede answered proudly.

'Everyone believes that story,' the Earthworm laughed.
'He's really only got forty-two.'

'Why are you all so big?' James asked.

'It was strange,' the Centipede answered. 'I was under
the peach tree when some little green things ran under
my nose. I ate one ...'

'Me too!' the other insects shouted.

'It's too late for stories,' the Old-Green-Grasshopper said. 'Miss Spider, will you make the beds, please?'

Miss Spider started work.

'I'll make yours from my softest thread,' she told the Old-Green-Grasshopper. 'James, would you like *your* bed hard or soft?'

'Soft, please,' James answered.

When every insect had a bed, James climbed into his. It was more comfortable than the hard floor at his aunts' house!

'Turn off the light!' the Centipede shouted at the ceiling.

James looked up and saw a giant flying insect.

'Good night!' the Glow-worm called, and the bright green light in its tail went out.

CHAPTER 4

'We're moving!'

James woke up suddenly, to the shouts of the insects.

'What's happening?' he asked.

'The Centipede is eating through the stem of the peach,' the Ladybird explained. 'When it breaks, the peach will roll down the hill, away from this horrible garden and your horrible aunts.'

The Centipede put his face through a hole in the ceiling.

'I've done it!' he cried. 'The journey begins!'

'But will it end in trouble?' asked the Earthworm.

'Of course not,' the Ladybird said happily. 'We're going to visit beautiful places and see wonderful things.'

Outside in the garden, James's aunts were standing at the gate.

'Look at the crowds!' Aunt Spiker said. 'We're going to make a lot of money today.'

'Where's that boy?' Aunt Sponge asked. 'He didn't come home last night.'

'Perhaps he fell in the dark and broke his neck,' Aunt Spiker said with a smile. 'What's that noise?'

They turned. The giant peach was moving quickly across the garden towards them.

They panicked. They screamed. They started to run. Then the peach rolled over them and continued down the hill. Behind it, James's horrible aunts lay dead on the ground.

When the giant peach rolled out of the garden, the crowds at the gate ran for their lives.

It crossed roads, and fields of cows.

Then, in a village, it rolled through the wall of a large chocolate factory and out the other side.

Almost immediately, chocolate ran out of the holes in the factory wall and down every street in the village. Children swam in it happily, and the chocolate ran into their open mouths.

The peach did not stop for anyone or anything. But then, at last, it dropped into the sea and floated quietly on the water.

CHAPTER 5

Inside the peach, James and the insects had a terrible time on that journey to the sea. They were on the ceiling, and then on the floor. They screamed in pain. But when the journey finally ended, they were silent.

The Glow-worm slowly put on the green light in her tail.

'I'll never be the same again,' the Earthworm said.

'But, dear friends,' the Old-Green-Grasshopper said, 'we're *there*.'

'Where?' they asked. 'Where's *there*?'

They helped the Centipede with his boots and Miss Spider made a ladder to the hole in the ceiling. Then they all climbed up it.

On top of the peach, the insects looked nervously around them.

'Where are the fields? Where's England?' they shouted.
'We can't swim!'

'Look – sharks!' the Earthworm said.

One shark bit a piece from the peach. Then other sharks attacked it too.

'They'll eat it all!' Miss Spider cried. 'Then they'll eat *us*. What can we do?'

'We need a lot of strong thread,' James said slowly.

'The Silkworm's downstairs,' said Miss Spider. 'She and I can make it. But what are you going to do?'

'I'm going to get this peach out of the water,' James said.

James quickly explained his plan. Not all the insects were happy about it, but they agreed to try. There were more and more sharks around the peach now.

Soon only the Earthworm was on top of the peach. He lay in the sun, with the end of his tail in the hole. Below, the Silkworm and Miss Spider were making thread as fast as they could. Just under the Earthworm, in the hole, James waited with a loop of thread in his hands.

A seagull looked down hungrily at the big fat Earthworm. Then it flew down towards him.

'Pull!' James shouted.

The Old-Green-Grasshopper and the Ladybird pulled the Earthworm's tail and the Earthworm disappeared down the hole. At the same time, James's hand went up and the seagull flew into the loop of thread. James pulled it tightly around the seagull's neck, and then tied the end of the thread to the stem of the peach.

'Next!' he shouted.

The Earthworm came up again and James hid with another loop of thread. They caught another seagull. And another. And another. And another.

'One hundred seagulls!' James shouted, and he tied the one-hundredth to the peach stem.

'More, James, more!' the insects cried.

'Two hundred!'

'Three hundred!'

'Four hundred!'

The sharks were really attacking the peach now.

'The Silkworm and Miss Spider are getting tired,' the Centipede shouted.

'They can't stop now,' James cried. 'Five hundred!'

He caught the five hundred and first seagull and tied it to the stem with the others. Suddenly, the giant peach started to rise out of the water.

It stopped. But then James caught the five hundred and second seagull, and the peach rose into the sky.

Everyone quickly climbed outside. They danced and shouted happily.

'Goodbye, sharks!' they cried. 'This is the best way to travel!'

'But how much of the peach have the sharks eaten?' James asked. 'We can't see from here.'

'I'll go down,' said Miss Spider.

She produced a long thread and tied one end to the stem. Then she jumped off the side.

The others waited nervously.

Minutes later, Miss Spider climbed back up the thread.

'The peach is fine,' she smiled. 'The sharks' mouths are too far back in their heads. They've only taken small bites.'

The *Queen Mary* was on its way across the Atlantic to the USA. The insects could see the ship, but not the surprise on the sailors' faces.

'Is that ball following us?' one sailor asked.

'It might be dangerous,' said a second man.

A third sailor looked through a telescope.

'There are birds everywhere,' he said, 'and there are giant insects on the ball. Yes, and a small boy in short trousers ...'

'Call the doctor,' the first sailor said to the second sailor. 'He's not well.'

Then the great round ball disappeared into a cloud.

The peach floated up into the highest clouds, and the Old-Green-Grasshopper started to move his back leg against his wing. He made beautiful music.

'Wonderful!' James said. 'What can *you* do?' he asked the Earthworm.

'Think of me when you stand in a field,' the Earthworm said.

'Plants grow better if the earth has passed through my body. Farmers love me.'

'And I eat the horrible little insects which kill their plants,' the Ladybird said. 'People love me.'

'They don't love *me*,' Miss Spider said sadly. 'But I don't hurt anyone.'

Then the Centipede sang a song.

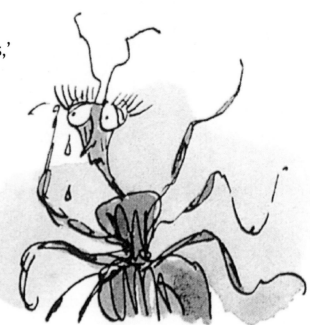

The Centipede sang another song. He started dancing wildly – and fell off the peach!

'Silkworm, more thread!' shouted James.

When the thread started coming from the Silkworm, James tied the end around his body.

'Hold the Silkworm,' he shouted to the others. 'I'm going down!'

And he jumped.

The insects cried.

'I don't mind about the Centipede,' the Earthworm said, 'but I loved that little boy.'

'Everyone, pull him up!' the Old-Green-Grasshopper shouted.

When they pulled James up, the Centipede's forty-two legs were tight around his body.

'Well done!' the Old-Green-Grasshopper said.

'But my boots are wet!' cried the Centipede.

CHAPTER 7

Night came. The threads between the peach and the seagulls shone in the moonlight.

They passed a big white cloud. Giant men were rolling small pieces of cloud into balls and throwing them off the cloud.

'Cloud-Men!' James realised. 'They're making hailstones!'

'But it's summer,' the Centipede said.

'Perhaps they're practising for winter,' James said.

Suddenly, the Cloud-Men noticed the peach and threw hailstones at it angrily.

James and the insects lay down quickly, but a hailstone hit the Centipede on the nose.

'Ow!' he screamed. 'That hurt!'

'Down the hole!' James shouted, and they all went inside.

After the peach moved away from the cloud, the travellers climbed up out of the hole.

'Look!' shouted the Ladybird.

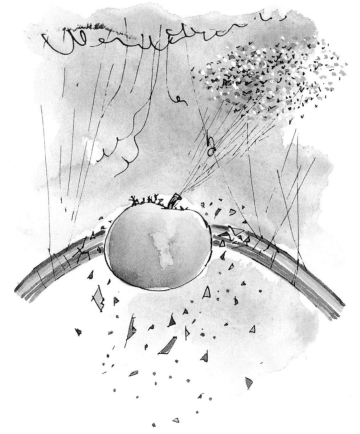

A great arch stood on a big cloud and reached high into the sky.

'Is it a bridge?' James asked.

'I don't know,' answered the Centipede. He looked frightened.

'But there are hundreds of Cloud-Men on it!'

The peach floated closer.

'They're painting it!' James cried.

In a few minutes, the arch was all the colours of ...

'A rainbow!' everyone shouted.

'Now they're sending it down to Earth,' James said.

'And we're going to hit it!'

And they did.

The rainbow broke, and the peach stopped moving.
The travellers panicked. James looked up at the angry faces
of the Cloud-Men.

One giant Cloud-Man jumped off his cloud. He reached for one
of the threads between the peach and the seagulls. Then he
started to climb down it.

'Help!' cried the Ladybird.

'He's going to eat us!' cried the Old-Green-Grasshopper.

'Centipede,' shouted James, 'bite through that thread!'

The Centipede ran to the peach stem and bit through the
thread. A seagull flew away, free at last, with a Cloud-Man
below it on the end of the thread.

Suddenly, the two parts of the rainbow fell towards the Earth, and the peach started to float away from the cloud. Cloud-Men ran along the cloud and threw things at the travellers. One threw thick purple paint.

The Centipede screamed. 'I can't see! And I can't move my legs!'

It was quick-drying rainbow paint.

'But you can still move your mouth,' the Earthworm laughed.

At last, the seagulls pulled the peach away from the cloud. Then everyone tried to help the Centipede.

'I know ...' said James. He stopped. 'Did I hear something?' he asked. 'Was that a voice – above us?'

Everyone looked up except the Centipede. He, of course, could not move his head. Above them was a large black cloud which looked very dangerous.

From high up on the cloud, a loud voice cried, 'Turn on the water!'

Then the cloud burst open and a great river of water fell on the seagulls and on the peach.

The travellers panicked. Some held the peach stem. Others reached for the threads. They could not speak or even breathe.

'This is the end of everything,' James thought.

But the seagulls pulled the peach through the water and out the other side.

'That was terrible!' the Old-Green-Grasshopper cried, when his mouth was empty of water at last.

'I'm clean!' shouted the Centipede happily. 'The paint's gone! I can move!'

'That's a pity,' said the Earthworm.

Now the seagulls were flying faster and faster, with the peach behind them. They passed through clouds where more Cloud-Men were at work – with snow machines and wind machines and machines for every kind of weather.

A giant animal with big, wide wings came down towards them out of the dark. It circled around them and made deep, sad cries. Then it flew away into the night.

'I'm frightened. When will it be morning?' Miss Spider asked.

'Soon,' James answered. He looked to the east. 'It's getting lighter over there already.'

They all sat silently and watched the sunrise.

When full daylight came, they stood up.

'Look!' shouted the Centipede. 'There's land below us!'

The others looked down. 'He's right!' they cried.

'Streets and houses!'

'The buildings are very tall!'

A thousand metres below them, a city shone in the early morning sunshine. Cars and people looked like little insects.

'It's not England,' the Old-Green-Grasshopper said.

'So where is it?' asked Miss Spider.

James was excited. 'Those buildings are skyscrapers!' he cried. 'So this is the United States of America. We've crossed the Atlantic, my friends!'

'Really? It's not possible!'

'I don't believe it! That's wonderful!'

'I've always wanted to visit the USA,' said the Centipede. 'I had a friend who ...'

'We don't want to know about your friend,' said the Earthworm. 'How are we going to get down to Earth?'

'Ask James,' said the Ladybird.

'It won't be very difficult,' said James. 'If we free a few seagulls – not too many, of course – we'll float slowly down to the ground.'

Far below them, in the city of New York, people were panicking. Everyone could see a great round ball, high in the sky, above the centre of the city. Was it a bomb? People started running everywhere.

Radio and television stations told everyone to go underground immediately. Planes flew up from Washington, DC, the capital city of the USA. People heard the terrible news in every part of the country, from Alaska to Florida, from Pennsylvania to Hawaii – the biggest bomb in the history of the world was above New York.

'Bite through the first thread, Centipede!' James ordered.

The Centipede bit through one of the threads and a single seagull flew away.

'Bite another!' James ordered.

'Why aren't we going down?' the Earthworm asked.

'The peach is lighter now,' James said. 'It lost some juice when the hailstones hit it. Cut away two more seagulls, Centipede! Ah, now we're going down. Don't bite any more. If you do, we'll fall too fast.'

Slowly, the peach lost height.

Then ...

wHOOOSH!

A plane flew just over their heads. It cut through all the threads, and the peach fell towards the Earth.

'Help!' cried the Centipede.

'Save us!' cried Miss Spider.

'Do something, James!' cried the Earthworm.

'I can't. I'm sorry,' said James. 'Close your eyes, everyone!'

The peach fell faster and faster. They all held tightly to the stem.

Down below them people watched, shocked, and thought of their families.

'The bomb is coming,' they thought. 'This is the end.'

The peach was not far from the buildings now.

'Goodbye, everyone!' James shouted.

Most of the skyscrapers had square tops, but the tallest building had a long, sharp point. And the peach fell onto the point of the Empire State Building.

CHAPTER 10

The news travelled quickly around New York – it was not a bomb. More and more people ran into the streets and looked up.

'There are *people* up there!' they cried. 'Men from Mars!'

'Or from the moon!'

Police cars arrived at the Empire State Building and six hundred police officers ran into the building. They went up in the lifts and stood at the bottom of the sharp point.

'Show yourselves!' an officer shouted.

The Centipede put up his great brown head and smiled his ugly smile. Some of the police officers fell to the ground in shock.

'What *is* that?' an officer cried.

'Where are you from?' another man shouted.

'From thousands of kilometres away,' shouted the Centipede.

'I was right – from Mars,' the man told his friends.

Then the Old-Green-Grasshopper put his head over the side of the peach, and six more officers fell to the ground in shock. But when there were *seven* giant heads above them, there was real panic.

Then, suddenly, the panic stopped, because a small boy was waving to them.

'Hello, everyone,' he shouted with a smile. 'We're very glad to be here. Don't be frightened. My friends aren't dangerous.'

The police brought a long ladder, and James and the insects climbed down it. Then a hundred men brought down the giant peach.

After James told his story, people clapped. 'Welcome!' they shouted.

They put James and his friends in a car, and drove them through the streets of the city. The peach followed on a lorry.

Suddenly, a little girl ran towards the car.

'Could I *please* taste your wonderful peach, James?' she asked.

'Of course!' James answered.

More and more children ran from the crowd. They ate all the delicious fruit and only left the stone.

The travellers did well in their new country. The Centipede, for example, became rich from a boot-making business, and the Glow-worm lit the torch of the Statue of Liberty.

The peach stone sat in Central Park, and it was the home of a very famous person – James Trotter. Every day, children knocked on the door and James welcomed them. Hundreds of children came, so the loneliest, saddest boy in the world had a lot of new friends. They all wanted to hear about his adventures.

So James decided to write a book – and you have just finished reading it.

Before You Read

❶ **This is James, before his adventures in this book. What do you think?**

  a How old is James?

  b What is round his neck?

  c What is in his suitcase?

  d What is happening to him?

  e Is he happy about it?

❷ **Match the names of the insects in the story with the pictures. How many can you guess? Use your dictionary.**

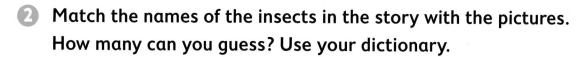

the Centipede   Miss Spider   the Ladybird   the Silkworm
the Earthworm   the Glow-worm   the Old-Green-Grasshopper

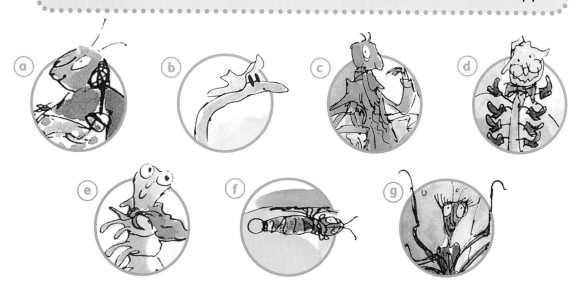

Activity page ❷

After You Read

1 **How do these happen? Explain.**

    a James is suddenly alone in the world.

    b A peach and some insects become giants.

    c James meets the insects for the first time.

    d Aunt Sponge and Aunt Spiker die.

2 **Look at the pictures. What is the problem, and how does James solve it?**

3 **Copy this table and complete it. What makes James happy when he is ...**

with his parents?	with his aunts?	with the insects?	at home in Central Park?
the beach			